I0766337

Black Hearts- *Loving From Our Wounded Places*

Table of Contents

Brown Eyed Girl

Dear Diary,

I was sneaking to the kitchen last night when I heard Nancy on the house phone. Nancy told her sister she hate she picked me out of all the other girls at the foster home. She said I was the worst thing that ever happened to anyone. If them people wasn't paying her she would've took me back. She said maybe my momma and daddy hated me that much they died in that car crash on purpose leaving me all alone as a baby.

I hate her! I hate it here!

***

"Open up! Open yo fucking legs, lil girl!" Dre's spit flew from his mouth onto Tina's face. The musk and boldness of his cologne made her nauseous.

"Please! Please don't hurt me, Dre!" Tina pleaded with tears streaming from her big, brown eyes. Dre ignored her cries as he pried open her legs. Tina tried to push Dre's body off her, but her twelve-year-old body was no match for a grown man.

"Shut the fuck up!" Dre put his hand over her mouth as he started to finger her vagina.

As she shut her eyes, the pain pierced her insides.

She was just another girl stuck in the foster care system. No matter where she was placed, a sense of emptiness always followed her.

If my daddy was here, could he protect me from Dre? she thought.

Dre was Tina's foster brother. *The monster and molester.*

Tina knew no one was coming to save her. Today was one of those days.

I wish I was dead.

The vintage stereo blared the voice of Norman Connors. *You areeeee my starship come take me up tonight. Don't be late.*

***

Tina was permanently stuck in a tiny, two-bedroom house with "Nasty Nancy" and her grown-ass son, Andre. Dre made her feel uncomfortable the day she walked through their gated door six years ago. He watched her every move. When Tina would walk in the living room, she would find his piercing, dark eyes staring at her. The hair on the back of her neck would stand. Dre invaded bath time when he would "accidentally" burst through the door. Tina's body would clam up as his eyes surveyed every part of her body. Tina never told "Nasty Nancy." She was afraid of her because she was verbally abusive. Nancy always blamed her for everything.

"Lil Girl why you got them lil shorts on?"

"I should smack the shit outta yo lil bald head ass."

Nancy wasn't going to save her from Dre; nobody was going to save her. Numbing her emotions was the only way to survive that house of horror.

6

Tina wandered aimlessly around the house for weeks.

"Girl, what the fuck wrong wit you? I swear yo ass is slow. You better get it together before your uncle come here," Nancy snarled.

Tina felt a slight smile across her face. She was excited to see her Uncle Joe. He was the only consistent family member in her life. Everyone else was like distant relatives she'd only heard about, but her daddy's brother loved her. Uncle Joe always told her how much she reminded him of his little brother. He said they had the same smile. Tina rushed to her room to get ready. It felt like only seconds before she heard the doorbell. She took off to the front door.

"Hey, baby girl!" Uncle Joe gave her the biggest hug and kiss on her forehead. "I got you some of them barbie dolls you like."

Nancy was standing in the corner, rolling her eyes. She was so jealous because no one ever gave her gifts. Tina hated when she stayed in the living room during their visits.

"Did you eat?" Uncle Joe asked.

"No!" Tina pouted.

"Girl, you gone sit there and act like I didn't make some greens?" Nancy put her hands on her hips.

Tina swallowed the lump in her throat. She knew to choose her words carefully. Nancy wasn't crazy enough to hit her in front of him, but Uncle Joe had to leave at some point.

"Oh, I think… I mean…I forgot I don't like greens." Tina held her head down in a whisper.

Uncle Joe lifted her head up. "Baby girl, you know Uncle gone take you to McDonald's. Go get yo shoes." Tina ran back to her room to grab her favorite pair of pink L.A. Gears.

As soon as they walked outside, Tina let out a deep breath. *I wanna go live with Uncle Joe.* It was a thought that never went anywhere. When she walked down the driveway, she saw Uncle Joe's blue Fleetwood Cadillac. Uncle Joe let her hand go so he could open the door. Tina never rode in the front of Nancy's old beat-up black Taurus.

"Here you go, baby girl." Uncle Joe slowly opened the door of his Cadillac.

When Tina got in the car, she rolled the window down. Uncle Joe reached over to turn the stereo on to play his old school slow jams. Tina let the breeze blow her big, puffy ponytail.

The Stylistics belted through the speakers. *First you love me, then you hate me.....that's a game for fools.*

***

Dear Diary,

Nancy always cussn me out. Dre keep hurting me. I wish I had a gun; I could pop myself in the head. But what if I don't die? Will I have to live with a messed-up face?

Uncle Joe's visits were the only thing keeping Tina from going with those ugly thoughts.

"Ayy little heffa, I need you to clean up this house. I'm about to have company." Nancy rushed into the room and lashed out.

"I just got home from school. I need to do my homework."

"Girl, I know you not back talking me!" Nancy spit.

"Ok!" Tina put her head down.

She knew enough not to argue with Nancy. There was no winning. Tina did as she was told and cleaned the house from top to bottom. The one good thing about cleaning was she could listen to music. If she had on headphones, no one could hear her sneak listening to grown folks' music. Tina grabbed the mop and pretended it was a microphone.

Karen White blared through the headphones. *Like a child on Christmas day…I was so anticipating AND I DIDN'T KNOW I could ever feel this wayyyyyyyyyyyyyyy. Love saw it…Love saw the change in my heart. You brought me so much joy.*

Music was her safe haven, a short escape from the sickness in that house.

***

Tina was so happy it was the weekend. She sat on the edge of her twin-sized bed, watching Stunt Dawgs. It was her Saturday morning ritual.

"We are the Stunt Dawgssssssssssssssss!" Tina yelled as she jumped up and down on her bed.

"Girl, shut the hell up!" Dre came crashing through the door. Tina laid back on the bed. "I'm just watching tv," Tina replied.

Dre inched closer to Tina so much she could smell the strong reek on his breath. Dre brushed his hand across her chest. Tina laid back and closed her eyes. *I hate you, Dre!*

As he rubbed her breasts, Tina slid her hand under her pillowcase. She reached for the kitchen knife she had stored there for some weeks. She didn't know how to use it, but she knew it would protect her. Hands shaking, she brandished the weapon.

"Don't touch me no mo!" *You got to fight back! Nobody else about to save yo ass!*

Dre's face turned white like he had seen a ghost. "Little bitch, you threaten me." Her tears turned into ice as they rolled down her cheeks.

"Imma kill you, bitch!" Tina spat. Dre must've saw the icy tears because he backed off and ran out the room. Tina heard his footsteps running through the house.

"Ma!" Dre screamed down to Nancy's room. "This little girl tried to touch my penis." Dre lied.

 Tina hid the knife and jumped out the bed. She ran down to Nancy's room to plead her case.

"He lying on me!" Tina cried.

"Little girl, what did you say? Did you just call somebody a liar in my damn house?" Nancy grilled her.

Tina couldn't get her words out fast enough. Nancy was fluent in the art of war. She kept the words coming, and they were cutting like a knife. Nancy ran to the phone and wrapped the long cord around her arm. She didn't even say hello before she started screaming into the receiver.

"Joe, you better come get this little hoe. I knew she was trouble walking around here in them little ass shorts. She got to get the fuck out my house now!"

Tina's body slumped over as she slid down the wall of Nancy's bedroom. Tina breathed for what felt like the first time in the twelve years of her life.

Please come get me, Uncle Joe.

Summer Madness

I can't believe it's been two years since I been here, Tina thought as she slid on her gold, dolphin hoop earrings and Turkish Link necklace. Tina grabbed a pair of red and white slouch socks to match her fresh Nike Cortez.

Tina was going to the store, but being fly was a necessity. She was that girl in the hood. Now that she was in high school, she had to up her wardrobe.

Uncle Joe's house was so different from being in hell with "Nasty Nancy" and Dre. Uncle Joe was strict, but he never hurt her.

"Ok! You cute." Tina looked at her body in the full-length mirror on the back of the bathroom door. Tina strutted out the house toward 7 Mile road so she could get some attention.

Cars honked as they drove past her. She sashayed her way to Rock's Corner store. As soon as she stepped foot in the door, the cashier gave her a big grin.

"Hey beautiful," he said. Tina rolled her eyes.

Rock old nasty ass. Ugh! Tina walked to the back of the store. "These snacks about to hit." Tina grabbed a bag of hot Cheetos and a bottle of Clear Fruit. "Ay, where the Now-N-Laters at?" she yelled up front to Rock.

"They up here, beautiful. You got to come see me." He flirted. Tina smacked her lips. *He better not play wit me.*

Tina slapped the crinkled five-dollar bill on the counter and rushed out of the store. She was moving so fast; she flung the door open and hit somebody.

"Damn baby!" an irritated voice said. Tina stepped around the door so she could put a face to the voice. She was ready to cuss somebody out. When she looked into his face, she saw his frown turn into a smile.

What the hell he smiling at with them crooked ass teeth?

"Excuse me, shit!" Tina snapped as she tried to push past him.

"Shit ma, calm down! You the one ran into me," he said in a deep voice as he folded his arms. "Wassup ma? Little feisty ass," Tone said with a little chuckle.

He pushed his chest up against hers. Tina got a whiff of his Calvin Klein's Eternity cologne.

"Don't touch me!" Tina screamed.

"Damn baby! You aight? I ain't trying to hurt you," Tone responded.

"Wassup?" She returned the question with an attitude.

"Ok, baby girl, what's yo name? Damn!" Tone said. Tone looked deep into her big, brown eyes. "Damn, you got some pretty ass eyes."

"It's Tina!" She popped her lips. She finally gave him a sneaky grin. *Is he for real? Do he think my eyes pretty?* Tina was always self-conscious about her eyes. "Nasty Nancy" teased her about one of her eyes being bigger than the other. Tina tried to get rid of him, but he wasn't leaving her alone.

Let me let this nigga walk me home so I can go on about my day. Uncle Joe house ain't too far if he tries to get crazy, she thought.

Tone and Tina got to the corner of Uncle Joe's house. "Ok, you can stop right here."

"What house you stay in?" Tone asked. "I been gone for a little minute but I know everybody over here. A nigga was on a little vacation if you know what I'm saying."

Tina pointed to the third house on the corner with the white aluminum siding.

"I stay wit my uncle," Tina said.

"I know that nigga Joe ain't yo uncle?" Tone laughed. "Ol' G is a nut, man." Tina laughed. She knew Tone was right. He put his hand on her chin. "Yeah, I'm gone let you go. I wanna see you again though. Just don't feel like dealing wit that nigga mouth right now. I respect the old heads."

Tina couldn't control her smile.

"Maybe you can swing by this weekend. We can hang out on the porch. Just know my cousins gone be there if you try to act crazy."

"Oh shit, cool! I know Keisha crazy ass already. I can call my niggas."

"How you know my cousin?" Tina rolled her eyes.

"I ain't no dirty nigga, baby. I wouldn't push up on you and yo family. Like I told you, I know everybody. This my hood!" Tone boasted.

Tina scribbled her number on her receipt and strutted off. Tone watched her walk away.

Lil Momma wearing the shit out them little biker shorts.

***

When Tina got into the house, she ran to the cordless phone. She was out of breath trying to dial Keisha's number.

"Bitch!" Tina screamed into the phone.

"Girl, calm the fuck down!" Keisha snapped. Keisha was the oldest out of the three cousins, but she was only a few months older than her sister, Nikki. Yeah, Uncle Joe was in them streets. Tina was too excited to even snap back.

"Girl, call Nikki on the three way," Tina demanded. She needed to tell them at the same time about Tone's fine ass.

"Girl, I know you not fucking around wit Tone crazy ass?" Keisha asked. "Everybody know that nigga ain't wrapped too tight," she rambled on.

"Girl, if my daddy find out…he gone kick yo ass. Tone too old for you anyway!" Nikki had to add her two cents.

Damn hoes! I don't plan on telling him my real age anyway. But that ain't ya'll damn business.

Tina rushed to change the subject.

"Just ask ya'll mommas if ya'll can come over on the weekend. We can go to this skate party at Northland," Tina said.

Uncle Joe never let her go to the westside by herself. It didn't matter that the westside niggas in Detroit were cool and laid back pretty boys. Tina knew her cousins was her only option to get there.

Tina grabbed her baggy, dark-rinsed Boss jeans, and a crisp white t-shirt. She wrapped the black and white bandana around her signature bun. The baby hairs were popping! She knew how to make that Pro-Style gel pop on her baby hair.

"Aye baby girl!" Tina heard Uncle Joe yelling from downstairs. She immediately rushed down the steps.

"Listen, ya'll know I gotta go to work at 4 a.m. I'm not picking ya'll asses up after 7. Now here go some money fo ya'll pockets!" Joe shot her a stern face.

Tina knew to just say yes and keep it moving. *It's time to have some damn fun,* she thought. ***

On the way to Northland, they picked up Nikki and Keisha. Tina was begging Uncle Joe to let them play their music in the car.

"I don't wanna hear none of that ruckus," Joe said.

"Please uncle," Tina begged.

"Please daddy." The girls pressured him.

"Put the shit in, but if it ain't right I'm throwing it out!"
Joe yelled.

Tina popped in the cassette. *We're JJ FADE and we here
to rock.*

The girls screamed. "Supersonic!!!!!!!"

"See that's it! I don't wanna hear that shit." Joe
was trying to turn the volume down. The girls knew not to push it,
so they rode in silence. Joe dropped them off at the front door of
the skating rink.

"Bye uncle, I promise we gone be good!" Tina yelled back
as she ran toward the door.

The line was around the building. Tina spotted a clique of girls
standing outside with their waterfall microwave ponytails. A few
guys were rocking Girbaud jeans.

"Damn, I see some fine dudes," Nikki said, flashing her
dimples.

"Girl, westside got them fine niggas." Keisha slapped her
sister's hand. They kicked it until they finally reached the front of
the line.

"Let's go grab some glow sticks," Tina said when they got
in.

As soon as they walked through the door, they heard the dj.
"All my backwards skaters report to the flo now!" he yelled into
the mic.

*I'll give you the Red Light Special..... Baby, it's yours, all
yours, if you want it tonight.*

"I love me some TLC! Ya'll already know I'm Chili. Look at the baby hairs boo boo!" Tina teased Nikki and Keisha. Tina was in her element.

"Damn baby, what's up wit you?" a guy yelled from the floor. He skated toward Tina and grabbed her hand. They took off hand in hand and slowly skated around the floor. Tina closed her eyes and smiled. She felt his hand slide across her ass.

"Stop!" Tina nudged his hand off her ass. He slowly moved his hands off her ass just to find his way back there.

"Boy, what the fuck you doing?" Tina started pushing the guy and wobbling on her skates. The guy was holding her hands down as she clawed at this face. She could hear Keisha screaming from the other side of the room. "Get the fuck off my cousin." Keisha came flying down the middle lane. Nikki rushed over and started stomping the dude.

Security came running over and grabbed the girls.

"Ya'll got to get out of here with all that noise acting real eastside. Ya'll from the eastside ain't you?" The security pushed them through the doors. Tina looked at her cousins.

"So, who gone call Uncle Joe?"

Keep You In Mind

Tina had to listen to Uncle Joe's lecture all the way home. As soon as she walked into the house, she ran to the answering machine. *I wonder if Tone called me.*

"Now, I can't never get you to move that quick when I ask you to do something. You not even about to be on my damn phone after what happened anyway," Joe said through pursed lips.

Tina pushed the red button on the little, black box. "I'm just checking it for you." Tina gave Uncle Joe an innocent look.

"You have one message," the voice spoke softly from the box.

"Hey Joe! It's Sheila." A woman's voice came through the machine. Joe ran to the box and pressed the stop button.

"Ohhhh!" the girls said in unison.

"Now look who running?" Tina said playfully.

Uncle Joe turned around and gave them that look. He never whooped them, but when he frowned up them eyebrows, they knew he was serious. The girls walked off to Tina's room. They bragged about how they jumped that dude.

"Girl, we beat his ass. Don't ever play with us. Let me put some music on so Unk don't hear us," Tina whispered. "He gone beat our ass if we wake him up."

Tina walked over to the stereo and cut on WJLB radio station.

Radio playing It's The Quiet Storm.

Tina turned the dial up about two notches. The girls looked at each other at the same time. They got up and started mimicking the singing group, Jade. Tina grabbed the hairbrush she used for them fire ass baby hairs as her mic.

You just won't seem to call...My mind is so confused, but you don't seem to care at all...

Keisha and Nikki frowned their eyebrows just like their daddy.

Tina was singing her heart out. She couldn't seem to get her mind off Tone at that moment.

Why this fool ain't called me yet? Is something wrong wit me? she questioned.

***

"Sheila gets on my nerves. She the only one leaving damn messages," Tina thought out loud. *She probably the reason why Tone can't get through.*

Tina was pacing and tapping her fingers on the kitchen counter. "I need to just hit up Robert. I'm not about to be sitting here looking crazy."

Tina had met Robert a few weeks before Tone. He would be a nice distraction for the moment.

Ring....Ring...Ring...

"Who dis?" Robert said in a low, sexy tone.

20

Tina laughed. "Boy please! Me and my cousins gone come over there in bout an hour." Robert had some fine ass brothers so this would keep them occupied.

"I can't wait to see yo sexy ass," Robert whispered. Tina rolled her eyes. *This fool putting it on extra thick.*

"Boy, ok!" Tina slammed the phone down.

"We got us a date ya'll!" she screamed up the stairs.

"Get ya'll butts up and get fly!" Tina already knew her white booty shorts were going to be the play for today. Like Sir Mix-A-Lot said, baby got back.

Tina watched as Keisha laid out her white pleated tennis skirt, white tee, and a fresh pair of off-white K-Swiss. Nikki was ironing her Karl Kani denim shorts.

"I might kill they ass today with these blue Nike Air Max. Look at the bubble gum sole?" Nikki said, as she pointed to the corner.

"Girl, we about to be out here like SWV!" Keisha said. Tina was definitely serving Taj with the long-wrapped hair. Keisha had an attitude like Lelee. Nikki was serving bossy like Coko.

When they stepped out of the house, the cars were pulling up left and right. The niggas were all up and down 7 Mile.

"Aye, booty shorts, lemme get yo number?"

"Redbone? Redbone, you gone act like you don't hear me."

"What up Doe, Chocolate? Wit yo sexy ass!"

They were so stuck on the dudes pulling up and exchanging numbers, they didn't notice the guy walking toward them.

"Damn!" Keisha jumped when he touched her shoulder. Tina swung her head around and locked eyes with the guy.

Muthafucking Tone! Tina felt her heartbeat outside of her shirt. Tone had a goofy grin on his face. *Raggedy mouth ass*, Tina thought to herself.

"Wassup, ma?" Tone grabbed Tina by her booty shorts.

This nigga got a lot of balls grabbing me like this and acting like he ain't have me waiting on him to call.

Tone turned around and spoke to Keisha and Nikki. Tone gave Tina this stern look. "I'm gone fall thru about 8 wit my mans and nem."

Tina turned her head to prevent him from seeing her smile. She was pissed right until he said he was coming over.

"Ok," Tina replied in a baby voice.

Tina talked about Tone all the way to Robert's house. *Damn, he smell so good. He know he fine as hell in that Guess hookup.* She knew it was gone be hard to entertain Robert after seeing Tone.

I just needed something to do and now I got something to do. I need to blow this joint.

As soon as they walked through the door, Robert was all in. "Boo, you want something to drink? You wanna go upstairs?" Robert was persistent. Tina was so annoyed that Keisha and Nikki left her alone because they were too busy entertaining his brothers.

This nigga really do look goofy with that high top fade. Damn, I never recognized it before, but Robert is a lame.

"You alright?" Robert asked.

"Man, I'm just hungry. I think I'm gone grab some Coney's," Tina said in a baby voice.

"You know I already got you," Robert mentioned eagerly.

Tina shot up. "I'll just hit you after." Robert was still talking when she walked to the back to grab Keisha and Nikki.

"Damn heffa! We just got here!" Keisha growled at Tina.

Tina smacked her lips. "Damn, I don't feel good." Tina had told about five lies in ten minutes. Keisha and Nikki got up reluctantly after Tina stomped her way through the house.

Once they got outside, Tina gave them the real.

"Robert could never be Tone. That nigga is whack. Let's hit up Rock's and grab some St. Ides. I heard they got a new flavor too," Tina said with excitement. Nikki looked at Tina.

"Nigga, you be big tripping but I'm down to get some drank. Yo ass betta grab some Coney's too so you don't get sick!"

"Here you go acting like you my damn momma." Tina hated it when they did that.

The girls ran across 7 Mile to hit Sugar & Spice burger joint. Nikki thought they had the best chili cheese fries on the eastside. Tina knew Robert's Coney Island had the best burger and chili cheese fries but she didn't feel like arguing. The girls sat, ate, and kicked it. As soon as they scarfed their food down, they went straight to Rock's. They were underage, but a little flirting would always get them what they wanted.

"Hey Rock!" Keisha batted her hazel eyes at him. Rock was flattered but he never took the bait.

"Girl, I'm not about to deal wit Joe's crazy ass! Now, what do you want, mami?"

Nikki interjected. "You already know what we want."

"Here you guys go again. Hurry up, grab it, and go!" Rock said in an irked tone.

The girls ran to the back of the store and grabbed a couple of bottles of St. Ides before they belted out. Tina knew Uncle Joe worked late on Sundays. Keisha and Nikki already asked their moms if they could stay one more day. The plan was in motion. It was time to get drunk and chill on the porch. The girls started flagging down cars and playing the game of getting numbers again. Nikki got a hit with some fine ass dark skinned dude in a white Caprice Classic.

"Damn heffa!" Tina said, scoping out Nikki from the porch.

"Yo ma!" Tina almost jumped out of her skin when she heard the voice. It was Tone's crazy ass coming from out the bushes. In eighty-five-degree Detroit summer heat, this fool had on a black hoodie. He was breathing heavily with a sense of urgency in his eyes. "I just jacked a fool. I need you to stash this for me." Tina saw the flash on the nickel-plated gun. She had seen one in movies but never up close.

"Huh? What I'm gone do with this?" Tina looked at him, confused.

"Damn, you ain't down?" Tone asked. Tina grabbed the gun from his hand.

"Good looking, ma." Tone kissed her forehead and ran off.

Shit! Tina thought as the sensation ran up her back.

Tina snapped out of it and ran into the house. She flew up the stairs and ran into her room. As she was placing the Glock under the mattress, she saw Keisha's K-Swiss.

"Bitch, are you dumb?" Keisha ranted. Tina jumped up and walked toward the bedroom door.

"Why you so damn nosey? I ain't even do shit!" Tina spat.

"You don't even know this nigga for real. He be in all kinds of shit. You already acting like you Bonnie and Clyde," Keisha ranted. Tina pushed past Keisha. Once Tina got back to the porch, she grabbed her St. Ides. Keisha came bursting through the screen door. Tina looked at Keisha.

"Bitch!" They burst out laughing.

A Love of Your Own

A few hours later, a black Regal pulled up in front of the house. *Who is that? Is that 5-0?* Tina instantly thought about the gun she stashed.

Tina's heart gained its normal rhythm when she saw Tone jump out of the passenger's side.

Tina then glanced over at a short, dark-skinned dude climbing out the backseat.

Damn! she thought.

A tall, lanky dude came from around the driver's side. They were all fine, but Tone did it for her. Tina felt starstruck as she stared at Tone walking toward her. The more she fought back her smile, the more her cheekbones jumped. Tone was smiling so hard; she could see the black on his gums.

"Hey." Tina opened her arms to hug Tone.

Tone leaned in and hugged her tight. "Damn, you soft as hell." Dennis interrupted their embrace.

"Nigga, this ain't no love connection." Everyone laughed except Tone. He turned around and gave Dennis this crazy ass look. Tina noticed the dark look in his eyes.

"We can go chill in the basement, Unk at work," Tina said in excitement, changing the subject.

"Cool! These my niggas Dennis and Mike." Tone introduced them to Nikki and Keisha.

Keisha whispered in Nikki's ear. "Now, see this hoe gone get us killed."

Nikki nodded her head. "Yeah, but girl they are kinda fly. I want to get up on the dark skin dude."

"Fuck it!" Keisha gave Dennis a little sneaky grin.

They ended up having so much fun drinking and cracking jokes. It was almost 3 a.m. when they finally left.

***

Tina thought about Tone all week. She couldn't shake the thought of his kisses and the attention he gave her. They hooked up a few times after that night, but it was their late-night talks that did it for her.

"Bae, you sleep?" Tone asked.

"Naw, I ain't sleep." Tina was sleepy as hell, but she didn't want to get off the phone.

Uncle Joe crashed through her door. "You on that phone all times of the night!" Uncle Joe started hollering. "You bet not be all googly eyes over no knuckle head ass boy. Tell ya little friend you got to go to bed."

"Uncleeee!" Tina blushed from embarrassment. Tina slid the phone under the pillow so Tone wouldn't hear him nagging. She couldn't wait until Uncle Joe went back into his room.

"Hey bae!" Tina put on a soft, sultry voice.

"Man, my damn pops be tripping too. I hate that shit. It's like he always fucking with my moms and shit. I don't know why she don't leave that nigga. I would kill that nigga over my favorite girl." Tone went on spilling his family issues.

Tina listened to what felt like Tone's secrets. She realized how much he loved his momma. That was a soft spot for her because she didn't know what that felt like to have a mom. She didn't know what to say, so she just listened until he got tired.

"Let's kick it tomorrow. I wanna see yo sexy ass," Tone spoke.

Yesssss! I'm gone see my man. Tina screamed in her pillow.

"Ok, I will slide through." Tina couldn't go to sleep fast enough to wake up to see Tone the next day.

***

Tone peered through the screen door, trying to hold back his smile as he watched Tina make her way across the street.

"You so damn pretty." He held the screen door open and grabbed Tina by the arm. He guided her through the house down to his basement. Tina was nervous. *Girl, we up in his house.*

Her stomach was queasy and she couldn't stop biting her lips. When they got to the bottom step, Tina looked around the basement. *Oh, this his bedroom.*

Tone walked over to the large floor model tv. "Listen, I'm happy to see yo fine ass but you not gone make me miss Martin. This the episode when he acting like my nigga, Nino, from New Jack City." Tone gave her a smirk.

"Boy, you tripping. I wanna see it too. So don't bother me." She rolled her eyes. They started play fighting as they sat down on the couch. Tina felt Tone's eyes burning a hole in the side of her face.

"What?" She turned slowly to look at him.

"Shit, ma, you just damn near perfect. A nigga's dream girl. Yo hair, yo eyes, and shit— body banging." Tone started rubbing her hair. "Damn, how much oil sheen you spray in yo shit?" he laughed. Tina cringed inside as she rubbed her hair.

"Boy, shut up!" She pushed him in his chest. Tina couldn't believe what she was doing next as she leaned in to give him a kiss. She was sucking his tongue and biting his lips.

"Hold up, ma!" Tone jumped off the couch and walked over to the stereo to pop in 12-Play cassette tape. Tina peeked at Tone as he removed his Nike cut off t-shirt. He climbed on top of her and kissed her forehead before drifting to her lips.

"Umm," he moaned at the taste of her cherry lip gloss. He lifted her crop-top over her head. As he unsnapped her bra, Tina's thoughts raced. Truth was that Dre's perverted ass tainted her sexual encounters.

Maybe this is what I'm supposed to do. I don't want him to be mad at me. I can't tell him no!

Tone licked her nipples, and her legs shook like Bambi. As his tongue moved over her body, she moaned even louder. The louder the moan, the more he smiled. Tone slowly lifted and walked over to grab the condom off the nightstand. He rushed to pull his basketball shorts off while biting the package of the condom. Tina's eyes got big as she looked at his dick.

"Come on." Tone grabbed her hand and led her to the other side of the room. He laid her down on the bed and climbed on top of her. Tone forcefully grabbed her breasts and started sucking them.

"Ouch!" Tina whispered in embarrassment, but Tone kept sucking.

Tone grabbed his dick and pushed….and pushed. The more he pushed, the more she dug her nails into his back.

"Shit!" Tone yelled. He became frustrated because he couldn't get in and she was scratching his back.

"Turn around and get on yo knees!" he demanded. Tears welled up in her eyes as she got on all fours.

Do like Dre taught you…Be a big girl! Take the dick!

Song Cry

Tina's days went from magical to a disappearing act. Tone hadn't called since the day she left his house. He left her to sit. *I thought this was what he wanted? Was it bad? Did I not do good enough?* Tina was too embarrassed to call Keisha and Nikki. *They gone mother me and tell me how stupid I am for losing my virginity to this nigga.*

Tina grabbed her favorite Toni Braxton tape and popped it into her Walkman. It was her escape from the pain. As she shut her eyes, the notes pierced her heart.

Seven Whole Days and not a word from you.....Seven Whole Nights.....And I'm just about through.

After what felt like hours, Tina had convinced herself maybe something was wrong with Tone.

Maybe he got in some trouble or in jail. Maybe that's why he ain't called yet. Tina dialed Tone's number. She dialed several times but there was no answer. *I have to go around there and check on him. I know something is wrong now.* Once she got dressed, she sprinted out of the house.

When she finally reached his porch, with sweat dripping down her face, she mustered up the strength to climb the four steps. Her hands shook as she knocked on the screen door.

The screen door creaked open, and Tina noticed an unfamiliar face.

"Is Tone here?" she asked in a panic.

"He's not here," the girl replied in a polite voice. "Tone went to pick up our baby," she spoke through the screen.

"Baby? Baby? What fucking baby?" Tina spewed spit out of her mouth. It was like someone punched her in the gut.

"Bitch, who are you? I'm his baby momma," the girl spat back. *Yeah bitch, who are you to Tone. Huh Tina? I guess fucking nothing.* Tina's thoughts took over where her mouth couldn't. With the little strength she had left, she ran off his porch.

***

A baby? How you got a baby with a bitch? Tina replayed the thoughts over and over in her mind.

"I got to tell somebody about this shit!" she yelled as she picked up the phone to call Keisha.

"Girl what? Let's go beat this bitch ass. It's on, on sight." Keisha was pissed. "And he a hoe ass nigga for that!" she huffed. Tina felt embarrassed, trying to hold back the tears as she sniffled.

"Bitch, I know you not over there crying over no sucka?" Keisha pressured her. Tina knew Keisha was right, but it didn't mean that it didn't hurt. Tina closed her eyes. *I wish she would stop.* The line clicking interrupted Keisha's rant.

"Girl, hold on," she said with a sigh.

"Hello?" Tina said.

"Speak to Tina," Tone said aggressively. Tina's hand froze as she tried to grip the receiver.

"Tina! I know that was yo ass popping up at my house."
Tone was livid. "How you gone pop up over my shit?"

Tina finally broke out of her trance because she just knew this
nigga wasn't trying to flip the script. Tina slammed the receiver
down.

Ring…Ring… Tina kicked the receiver onto the floor.

Fuck him…. Fuck Keisha…Fuck that baby.

***

Tina and Tone's summer romance sizzled off. It hurt Tina like hell
to walk away, but it hurt more every time she thought about the
"little family" he had.

Lucky for her, her darkness was turning into light because school
was starting. School was one thing she didn't play about. It was
her dream to go to college. During the fall, she got her license and
started driving. Uncle Joe let her borrow his new Chrysler LeBaron
when she wanted to hang out.

Tina had a new kick it buddy from school named Renee.
From the first day of school, they just clicked. It was something
about Renee's attitude that Tina loved. Renee and Tina hung out at
all the high school parties. Renee was a free bird. She didn't care
about shit, which meant she never cared about getting caught.

"Girl, let's hit up this skip party this nigga throwing that go
to Osborn High School," Renee urged.

"Naw, you know I'm all about kicking it, but I don't do
skip parties heffa." Tina tooted her lips.

"Look, you know yo ass ain't gone miss them assignments. You are already on the honor roll. Just do something different this one time. Damn, nigga!" Renee was pleading her case.

"Ughhhh!" Tina pulled at her braids, tapping her foot. "Ok, but bitch if we get caught, I'm beating yo ass." Tina gave Renee a quick lecture.

Tina and Renee snuck over to this guy Timo's house. Tina prayed no one saw her as she parked the Lebaron in front of the house. *Uncle Joe don't play that shit about missing school.* When they stepped into the house, Tina asked if they had any alcohol.

"Oh, we got St. Ides for sure, some Boone's Farm." Timo was trying to finish his sentence before Tina interrupted him.

"Oh, some Boone's will do." Tina was eager to calm her nerves.

"Ya'll can move around. It's plenty in the kitchen." Timo pointed toward the back of the house. She left Renee in the living room as she filtered her way through the house to the kitchen. It was a guy sitting at the card table in the kitchen. He had the curliest black hair. The boy looked up with the prettiest smile.

"You want me to pour you a drink." He smiled. His smile captured Tina.

"Yeah!" She smiled back excitedly as she grabbed a chair from the table.

"My name Shard." He winked.

"Is that your real name?" she quizzed him. He gave a little chuckle.

"Naw, it's Rashard. You can call me whatever you like though."

Tina and Rashard exchanged numbers that day. After kicking it for a few weeks, it felt like Tina had found a good friend. Rashard was the total opposite of Tone from his looks to his lifestyle. He used his allowance to take her out on weekends, and he wasn't robbing people like Tone. Rashard was fun. They would hang out at the Butterfly and go-kart racing.

On one of their Friday night dates, Tina suggested they go to her favorite spot, Robert's Coney Island.

"Bet, I'm in," Rashard said eagerly. He wasn't about to pass up a Robert's Cheeseburger Deluxe. When they arrived, it was empty. Tina smiled at Rashard. They walked up to the counter.

"Lemme get a cheeseburger deluxe wit chili and cheese on the fries. Yo make that squeeze cheese!" Tina ordered.

"Let me get the same but put slice cheese on mine." Rashard gave Tina a devilish grin.

"You already know slice is the best, baby," he said in a playful tone.

They walked toward their favorite booth in the back. While waiting for their food, they heard a loud group of people walking in.

"Dang, they are so loud! Can you make it a carry out?" Tina asked in extreme annoyance.

"Not a problem." Rashard grabbed her hand and led her to the front. That's when they came face to face with the rowdy crowd.

"Who dis nigga?" Tina heard the words but couldn't see through the crowd. She was ready to fight.

"Who the fuck you—" Tina couldn't finish her sentence fast enough before she came eye to eye with Tone. His eyes were piercing red.

"Who is this nigga?" Tone grabbed the collar of her Nautica jacket.

Rashard stepped in between them. "What you doing, homeboy?"

"Nigga, who the fuck you talking to? This my bitch!" Tone was like a Pitbull.

Tone lifted his shirt and pulled the Glock from his waistband. He put the steel to Rashard's head. The waitress screamed through the Plexi-glass. "I'm calling the damn police!"

One guy in the crowd grabbed Tone.

"Nigga, let's go!"

"Let me catch you with this El DeBarge looking ass nigga in my hood again," Tone spat.

Tina hugged Rashard. "I'm so sorry…he ain't even my boyfriend." She cried.

"Let me go!" He shrugged his shoulders. They rode home in silence.

The steel of the gun and Tone's eyes flashed through her mind. Rashard was a square compared to Tone, but he still had feelings. When they arrived at her house, Rashard turned and looked her dead in her eyes.

"Lose my number."

You're The Key To My Heart

Why he doing this to me? I wasn't the disloyal one. The nigga took my virginity and played me. Then had a baby on me. Tone had called a few times since that night, but she refused to take his call until that point. The more she sat in front of the tv listening to BBD, the more it pushed her to get answers. Ronnie, Ricky, and Mike sang with their souls. *Tell me when will I see your smile again.* Tina rushed over to grab the phone. *I need some fucking answers now.* Her hands trembled as she dialed Tone's number by memory. Every ring increased the beat of her heart.

"Wassup?" Tone answered in a stern voice.

"It's me," Tina replied.

"Listen ma, who the fuck was that nigga?" Tone interrogated her.

"How you gone ask me about him and you got a baby?" Tina tried to fight back the tears as her voice crackled.

"Listen ma, meet me in the hood. I need to see you. Come by Mike's crib at 6." Tone was calm now.

"Alright!" Tina slammed the phone down.

When Tina hung up the phone, the tears stung her face. She gave herself a headache trying to think about what she needed to say to him.

I can't let him play me like this. I need to do something to get my mind right.

Tina sat on the floor, looking up at the ceiling until she noticed it was getting dark.

"Shit, what time is it?" She looked at the clock on the wall. "I got about an hour to get my shit together and confront this fool." Tina hyped herself up. *You ain't got to take shit this nigga giving you. He the one that's on some bullshit,* her inner thoughts screamed.

Once she got her courage up, she drove a few blocks to get to Mike's house. "If he gets crazy, Mike better check his ass," Tina whispered to herself in the car. Tina jumped out of the car and pulled up her low-rise jeans. She had no clue Tone was watching her from the window.

"Fine ass!" Tone whispered as he watched her hips swaying.

Tina walked up to the porch and rang the doorbell. Tone walked to the door and tried to play it cool.

"Wassup? Let's go to the basement," Tone demanded. He reached out and grabbed Tina's hand and she followed him downstairs.

Now girl don't get here and forget what he did to you. We need some damn answers.

She was cool until she looked at him. That stupid feeling was back.

Girl look at this man. He is so fine. "Get it together girl," Tina said.

"What you say, bae?" Tone asked.

Tina cleared her throat. "Oh, I ain't say nothing, bae."

Tone tried to make small talk, but Tina cut him off. She quickly snapped out of the trance and remembered the face of his girlfriend.

"Look, you been moving dirty, and I don't like that," Tina snapped with an attitude.

"Look, I know a nigga fucked up. I should've told you about my young dog. I had a girl before we met. Shit was rocky, ma! When she got pregnant, I had to man up. I ain't no slimmy nigga, I had to take care of mines. That day you popped up and shit she was just visiting," Tone said, looking into her eyes.

Her jaws were clenched, but her heart was saying go to him. Tone grabbed her hand while he talked to her. "I fucked up," he said with sincerity. Tina had never seen him like this.

"Come here! Fine ass! You know I can't stay mad at you." Tone touched her face and kissed her forehead. Tina kissed him with every passionate bone in her body. Tone ripped Tina's shirt, trying to get it off. Tina pulled down her jeans and exposed her thong. It drove Tone insane.

"Damn baby," he let out a whisper. He pulled her panties to the side and rammed his dick inside of her.

"Daddy!" Tina screamed loudly. Mike ran to the basement door.

"Yo, ya'll good and shit?"

Tone moaned, "We good."

Mike was still at the door, but Tina didn't care. "Nigga, I know you not fucking in my basement!" Mike yelled. Tina and Tone couldn't stop. It felt way too good to stop. Tone grabbed her neck and they both came.

"Love you, ma!" Tone said. Tina was trying to catch her breath and make sure she wasn't going crazy.

Did this nigga just tell me he love me? Tina thought. She wasn't going to ask him. Tone kissed her forehead. Tina laid her head on his chest. She felt his heartbeat.

I missed you, bae.

Sabotage

I got my man back, Tina thought as she rubbed Tone's neck. She sat in the passenger's side as he rode to the spot. Tone told her he had a new business deal to make and needed her to ride along. He had been making moves and including her in every step.

"You know I like that shit. Nigga love them soft ass hands, bae." Tone smiled like a little boy.

Tina was feeling the butterflies again. When they pulled up to the spot, the house looked abandoned. The grass was tall, and the windows were blacked out with garbage bags. A guy came walking from behind the house toward the car.

"What up, boss man?" The guy smiled at Tone.

"Wassaup, my nigga, you ready?" Tone asked.

"Hell yeah! Let's get this scrilla." Tone was geeked up. He pointed toward Tina. "This my baby momma right here, Tina."

"I ain't know you had another baby." The guy looked confused.

"She don't know it either but she gone be." Tone laughed and slapped hands with the guy. Tina was all giddy like a little girl. *His baby momma.*

Once they got inside the house, Tina watched as Tone started bagging up little bags of white stuff. Tone told her to hold the brown paper bag full of money. Tina didn't ask questions, she just stuffed it into her tiny Baby Phat purse.

That day was just the beginning of what Tina felt like Bonnie to his Clyde.

***

After they left the spot, Tina tried Tone's burner phone several times. *He must be still out there hustling. I got to stop acting like a little girl. Maybe, I need to go see him instead of calling and nagging him,* she told herself.

Tina decided to ride past Dennis' house first to see if Tone was there. Tina spotted a group of guys standing in the driveway. She circled the corner and doubled back. When she hit the corner, she flicked her lights. Tone noticed a car riding up without lights. He immediately grabbed his strap. He was prepared to shoot the car up, but it looked familiar.

I know that ain't Tina, he thought. Tone's soldiers were in position to shoot. "Aye, chill!" Tone snapped. When the car was in full sight, he noticed the license plate on the front. It was Tina's crazy ass.

"What the fuck is she doing?" Tone whispered. She noticed Tone running to his whip. Tone hopped into his car and took off. He was on her ass. Tina's heart was pounding at a rapid speed.

"I can't pull over now this nigga gone kill me!" she yelled as she beat the steering wheel. Tone was riding her bumper so hard.

"Fuck!" Tina sped up and slid down a side street. She hit the alley and turned her lights off. Her heart was pounding out of her chest. She could see his car riding up and down the block.

"Where the fuck yo crazy ass at?" Tone was sweating feverishly. "I ain't got time for this silly shit."

Tina waited patiently for what felt like forever. Once she regained normal breathing, she turned her lights on. *What just happened?* Tina pulled slowly off and drove to Keisha's house.

"I can lay low over here. He not about to come acting crazy over here," Tina said through shallow breaths.

***

Tina flew up into Keisha's backyard. She pulled her car behind the house. Tina knocked on the door like she was the police.

"Who the hell is it?" Keisha's momma asked. *Damn, I woke auntie up,* Tina thought. *Let me get my shit together.*

"Hi auntie, It's me Tina," Tina replied in a sweet, baby voice. Diane opened the door. "Girl, what are you doing out this late?" she quizzed Tina.

"I just needed to get out. Can I please see Keisha?" Tina pleaded.

"Girl, yeah but you ain't got long," Diane replied.

Tina walked through the hallway to Keisha's room fast. She rushed through the door. Keisha was hanging up some Word Up magazine posters on her wall. Keisha jumped.

"Girl, what you doing here? My momma let you in?"

"I need you, bitch!" Tina rambled. Tina told Keisha about what happened.

"Bitch, are you crazy? You know that nigga is a nut," Keisha snapped. Tina knew she was right, but she just wanted to see him.

***

When Tina woke up the next day, she knew she was in trouble. She held her breath as she checked her voicemails. Tone had left a million voicemails. *"You need to call me back right the fuck now!"* She could hear the anger in Tone's voice. He wasn't even saying correct sentences.

"You now who did is! Call me." Tone's voice was full of rage.

I fucked up, she said to herself. There was no coming back from last night.

Tina called up Renee so she could assess the damage.

"Hey Re," Tina spoke softly into the phone.

"Girl, the whole hood was talking bout yo ass. What were you thinking rolling up on Tone like that?" Renee questioned.

Tina wanted to curl up in a ball and die. She was so embarrassed and now she was the gossip of the hood. Tina was dying inside and zoned out from the conversation. However, Renee said something that caught her attention.

"Wait, what did you say?" Tina paused. In the middle of all the gossip, Renee mentioned Tone was moving.

"Girl! Are you listening? Tone and his wife moving out to the burbs," Renee said. The pain was reminiscent of the day she sat on the porch listening to the bitch mentioning he had a son. *Did she just say his wife?* Yet, she was too embarrassed to ask Renee. *What did I do to deserve this, Tone? I thought you loved me,* Tina thought.

It finally hit her the reason it was hard to get a hold of him in the first place. *This nigga is married and playing house. He is too busy being a family man.*

"Hey girl, I got a call. Let me call you back!" Tina rushed Renee off the phone.

When Tina hung up the phone, she cried. Uncle Joe could hear the hurling from her screams.

"Baby girl?" Uncle Joe had walked into her room.

"Baby girl, don't tell me it's that boy again? You got to let him go!" Uncle Joe pleaded. For the first time, Tina took in the truth.

End Of The Road

Tina spent the next few months trying to move on. She learned from another hood reporter that Tone had gotten married some time ago. She didn't want to hear it, but she needed the truth. The truth just wasn't in Tone. Tone's lies ran its course. Tina sat in her reality as she waited outside her guidance counselor's office. It was time for her to get serious and set some goals. She was a senior now and needed a plan for her future.

"Hi, Ms. Thomas," Tina greeted her guidance counselor.

"Hello, Miss Jones! I'm so glad to see you. I really want to discuss what we talked about last year. I know you discussed wanting to be a teacher," Ms. Thomas said.

"Yes! I want to be an elementary school teacher so bad. I really want to help kids that look like me. Kids that went through a lot of shit. Opps! I'm sorry, Ms. Thomas," Tina said shyly.

"It's okay! I will let it slide today. I know you are deeply passionate about these things. Well, I have some great news. We have a college scholarship for teens that were once in foster care. You will get a full ride to whatever school of your choice. I think this would be great for you considering your circumstances," Ms. Thomas informed her.

"Are you for real? So, I wouldn't have to pay for anything?" Tina spoke with the biggest grin on her voice. It was like Christmas in May. She wanted to soak it all in. *We finally got some good news, girl.* Ms. Thomas looked her in the eyes.

"Baby girl, it doesn't matter where you've been. All that matters is where you are going."

Tina received her educational plan and prepared to get busy.

***

"Keisha and Nikki out living it up. I'm sitting over here reminiscing about this fool that ain't even my man no mo," Tina said out loud. She pulled out her old diary to write in. The phone rang and caught her off guard. She was talking all that shit, but she secretly hoped it was Tone. *Maybe he finally calling to apologize,* she thought to herself.

"Wassup, ol' lady? I see you still in the house being sad over that nigga," Keisha teased. Tina was afraid of being hurt again.

"Girl, shut the hell up! Ain't nobody thinking about that fool. Get auntie car and come scoop me!" Tina said.

"Bet, ol' lady!" Keisha said in excitement.

Tina hopped in the shower and turned on some music. When she jumped out of the shower, she ran to her closet. It was time to go all out. She heard Keisha's voice in her head *"Ol' Lady."* Tina grabbed the shortest shorts and smallest top she could find. She pulled her braids up into a ponytail. Tina got the idea from a Salt-N-Pepa's video.

Alright, let's have some fun, girl. She was dancing in the mirror when she heard the horn blow.

"Damn, Keisha must have been on two wheels!" Tina cracked up. She grabbed her bag and ran to the car. Keisha and Nikki were both in the car.

48

Keisha was blasting *Bone Thugs n Harmony*. They were some cuties, but they loved gangsta rap.

They started singing along to the song, *"Foe tha Love of Money…………"*

Tina was so happy that Keisha convinced her to go out. Keisha had met this guy named Craig.

Craig had introduced his brother to Nikki, and he wanted Tina to meet his cousin. They met up and went to the movies.

"Yall, what is this dude like? You know I'm not really trying to meet another sucka," Tina spoke.

"Girl, you just got to relax and see. He ain't Tone that's fa sho," Nikki responded.

Once they arrived at Bel-Air Movie Theater, Tina spotted the guys. *I hope it's the guy in the middle.* The guys started walking toward them.

"Hey, how you doing?" The guy extended his hand. *Okkkk, I guess this one mines.*

Tina let her guard down. She forgot what it felt like to laugh, and she needed it. She was having a blast with Craig's cousin, Red. Red was tall, light skinned with a low fade. *Red is fine! We could make some cute babies.* "Sis, you are thinking way ahead of yourself," Tina checked herself.

Tina and Red exchanged numbers so they could hang out again. In that moment, she wanted something different like that real love that Mary J. Blige rapped about.

***

Tina called Red up a few days later so they could hook up.

"Hey, Ms. Lady!" Red answered the phone. He made Tina smile, and she liked that.

"Hey Red!" she whispered in a soft voice. "I was trying to see what was up for today. I was thinking maybe we could go out to eat and then hit Blockbuster to grab a movie. My uncle is out of town. We could chill at my house," Tina suggested.

"I'm down for whatever you want, lady. I can pick you up around five. Just shoot me the address," Red said.

"Ok, I'm on the eastside. I know you said you lived west," Tina said.

"Oh, that's right! Shit, I got to go on MapQuest to look you up." Red laughed.

"You real funny, sir! I'll see you later," Tina snickered.

Tina felt a little excited about her date. Red was nice when she met him. *I hope this dude is a good guy for me.* Tina rushed to get dressed before Red came. She grabbed some Nike shorts, a cute sports bra top, and clean Nike Prestos. *We cute but we ain't doing too much.*

Tina sat on the porch patiently waiting for Red. She was enjoying the evening breeze when Red pulled up in a red BMW. He was older than her by three years. She didn't feel the need to lie to him about her age since this was her last year of high school. Red stepped out of the car with a huge grin.

"Hey, pretty lady!" Red said. Tina leaned back and enjoyed the view. Red leaned down and greeted her with a light hug. It impressed Tina that he didn't push up on her.

"Let's go! Don't want you sitting on this concrete." Red grabbed her hand, and they walked toward the car.

While riding to the restaurant, they got to know one another. They talked about music and playfully fought about their top rapper.

"The best rapper ever is Ice Cube." Tina smacked her lips.

"Little momma, what you know about Ice Cube?" Red laughed. "I bet you don't know about the Bop Gun," Red quizzed.

"Sir, please!" Tina laughed. Tina started singing *One Nation Under A Groove*. Tina immediately went into rapping Ice Cube's part. "If you hear any noise, it's just me and the boys playing with the toys…………Hit you with da BOP GUN!" Tina was enjoying his company. It felt like she'd known him forever.

When they arrived at Pizza Hut, Red opened the door for her. *Ok he a little gentleman.*

When they sat down, she caught Red staring at her. It gave her a weird feeling. She was feeling butterflies. Tina made small talk to break the awkward moment.

"Have you been here before? I love their personal deep-dish pizza and wings," Tina conversed. "You seem mad cool." He looked at her. They ordered their food and engaged in more conversation.

"Ok ma, tell me about your ex. I know you had a man or shit do you have a man now," Red said.

Tina almost spilled her water. She hated talking or thinking about Tone. It was the past, and she wanted to leave him there.

"Well, it's not much to talk about. He was married and never told me. End of story." Tina slightly rolled her eyes.

Red looked at her, confused. "Oh wow! He sounds like a clown." Red laughed.

For the first time, Red turned Tina off. She could hate Tone's guts, but no one could speak ill of him. Tina let out a sigh as she crossed her arms. Red must've noticed her body language because he quickly changed the topic.

"Alright, tell me what you want to do when you graduate." Red sat with his hands crossed.

That's more like it nigga. "Well, I just spoke to my guidance counselor. I can get a full scholarship to any school I want. I might go to either Wayne State or Michigan State. My dream job is to be a teacher." Tina got excited again.

"That's so dope. So, you smart, huh?" Red said.

"Of course!" Tina smirked.

"Alright, lady! I feel you. Let's hit this Blockbuster before they close. Tell me where to go though. You know I ain't from this side. West is the best!" he chuckled.

"Aight! Don't get messed up, boy." Tina gave him a serious face.

"Aight, Aight, Aight! Calm down, little momma," Red responded.

As soon as they got to Blockbuster, Tina ran straight to the back to grab her movie. Tina was excited to watch *Boyz n the Hood* for the millionth time.

"Bingo!" Tina shouted when she saw the cover.

"Damn that was quick. Alright let's go then." Red touched her back and led her to the checkout counter.

They drove in silence on the way back to Tina's house. Tina was enjoying Red's playlist of recorded slow jams. The Harman Kardon speakers blared the voice of Norman Connors. *You areeeee my starship come take me up tonight. Don't be late. My starship come take me up tonight.* Tina felt like her chest had tightened into a knot. It was like someone placed her in a chokehold.

"Cut that off…..cut it off!" Tina screamed at Red.

"Damn, you okay? You don't like old school music?" Red looked perplexed. He didn't understand but her face said a lot. "Alright, let me put on some rap then."

Tina sat in silence the whole way to the house. *I need to get home. I need to get home and relax.*

When they arrived back at Tina's house, Tina ran up the steps. *I need to put this movie on and just relax. I can just chill. I don't want him to think I'm crazy.* Tina took the movie out of the case and slid it in the VCR. She grabbed the remote and turned the volume up.

"I like talking to you." Red looked into her eyes.

"I like talking to you too," Tina said bashfully.

The movie was on, but they mostly talked. Tina felt comfortable. She looked over at Red and he grabbed her face. He leaned in and kissed her passionately.

Ok, I wasn't expecting that.

She was shocked because he seemed to be a square. Tina enjoyed his tongue. The sensation ran through her body. Tina's body felt feeble. Red's hand was creeping up her shirt and unstrapping her bra. Tina was lost in the moment.

Red went from slow to fast. He leaned on her and pressed his dick up against her. Tina felt his dick through his jeans. *Ok girl, what are we doing?* She liked Red, but this was going way too fast. Tina asked Red to slow down, but he must didn't hear her.

"Red, please stop. I don't think I'm ready for this," Tina whispered. Her whisper eventually turned into a scream. Red wasn't stopping. He ripped down her shorts. She attempted to fight him off, but Red was relentless. Tina laid there motionless as Red rammed his dick into her. She couldn't believe what was happening.

"Help me?" Tina's voice made a sound, but she couldn't scream anymore.

Red didn't last long. He pulled out and nutted on her legs. Red sat on the couch like nothing happened. Tina was scared. Her body was convulsing and shaking uncontrollably. Red finally broke the silence.

"Damn, that was good. Baby, I knew you needed that. I could tell cause you was tense," Red stated casually. Red walked over to the bathroom. "Ya'll got some towels?" Red yelled.

Tina sat as if her body was glued to the sofa. *You a fool for thinking a nigga could love you.* Red walked out of the bathroom and started talking again, but Tina was zoned out.

"I'll call you later." Red walked away.

Always In My Heart

"Little girl, tell me why that damn school called my job today. Ms. Thomas told me you been skipping class. They about to expel yo ass. Now, why you ain't been to school?" Uncle Joe was tearing her a new asshole.

God, just take me away!

"Do you hear me talking to you, lil girl?" Uncle Joe nudged her. "I know you not sneaking around with that little nappy head boy, Tone."

"Uncle, I'm sorry! I don't know. I just be tired." Tina's body shifted back and forth.

"Tired? You tired? Girl, I get my ass up every morning at 4 a.m. to work. And you talking bout you tired? If you don't get yo ass back in school, you can't be here?" Uncle Joe was furious.

"Alright." Tina just let the tears flow. *I really wish you knew, Uncle. But I know you gone kill me for having a boy in the house. Maybe the shit is all my fault.*

Tina's mind battled thoughts of anger to sadness.. She was so embarrassed and didn't want anyone to know, not even her cousins. Tina made up a lie about why she stopped talking to Red. He had called her a few times and left voicemails. Tina refused to answer his calls. She couldn't believe she was raped or the fact the person acted like it didn't happen.

Tina took days… weeks… to be alone in her room. It was the safest place for her.

 It was in her room that she heard Ms. Thomas' words during their meeting. *"Baby girl, it doesn't matter where you've been. All that matters is where you are going."*

Those words ushered her to get through the last month of school. She pushed past the pain to complete the assignments she needed to get her grades up.

Come on Tina, you can do this!

***

"I told you that you could do it." Ms. Thomas grinned at Tina as she handed her the diploma.

"I did it, Ms. Thomas. I did it!" Tina jumped with joy. Tina grabbed her diploma and looked back at Uncle Joe. In that moment, that was all she needed to see. He had the biggest grin on his face. *I ain't never seen him smile like that.* Tina walked off the stage and straight to Uncle Joe.

"Alright, baby girl, we gone party tonight." Uncle Joe smiled.

"I can't wait!" Tina did a little two-step dance. Uncle Joe had Keisha and Nikki plan everything out for her. *I got a few hours. I just need to hit the mall real quick. I need to be all the way fly*, Tina thought. After the graduation ceremony, she called up Keisha and Nikki.

"I have to get to the mall ASAP! Girl, the new Jordans dropped today," Nikki said.

"You already know I got the hook-up at Footlocker," Keisha boosted.

"Meet up at Eastland in front of Footlocker. I will be there in about a hour." Tina hung up the phone, bolted home to change her clothes, and ran to the mall. When she got to the mall, she spotted Nikki and Keisha waiting in front of Footlocker.

"They better have my damn size too," Nikki said as they walked into the store.

In the middle of her sentence, Nikki grabbed Tina's arm so hard that she almost fell. Tina looked up and looked directly into the eyes of the devil. *You dirty BITCH!* Nikki on the other hand was excited to see him.

"Oh my God, hey Red," Nikki said as she embraced Red.

"What up cuzzo?" Red responded. *Just breathe…. Just breathe!* Tina mouthed in between breaths. Red tried to hug Tina, but she pulled back. It was one thing to tolerate his voice, but she couldn't let him touch her ever again. Once the nightmare was finally over, they walked out of the store.

"Girl, Red is so fine. He's such a good dude. I can't believe you let him go," Nikki said.

Tina was ready to slap her. "Bitch he raped me!?" Tina wanted to yell out so badly but she did her infamous move and changed the subject.

"Let's get some pizza. I'm starving," Tina said in a whiny voice.

Keisha started telling one of her infamous stories on the way to the food court. When they reached the food court, Tina's jaw dropped.

She immediately spotted Dennis in a crowd. They were talking loudly and cracking jokes. Tina tried to gain control of her breathing again.

Lord, please don't tell me Tone here. I can't take any more surprises today.

The guys noticed the girls walking over to them. Dennis stopped Tina and started smiling. *What the hell he smiling for?*

"Wassup ladies?" Dennis smirked. He walked over and gave them a hug. She was starting to think the mall was a bad idea. Tina was still unsure whether Tone was there. She definitely wasn't going to ask. They kicked it and eventually headed toward Sbarro Pizza. She was so happy to dodge that bullet. *Whew, I'm so glad that fool ain't here.*

Dennis never realized how fine Tina was before. He needed to see if Tone was over this girl. Dennis grabbed his phone and dialed Tone's number.

"Yo!" Tone yelled into the phone.

"My man, one hundred grand. I just seen little momma you use to fuck with. Damn, what's her name?" Dennis was acting clueless.

"Nigga, don't call me bout no hoe!" Tone snapped.

Dennis replied, "I feel you my nigga, but she was looking good as hell. I was gone see if you was done wit her. I was bout to holla. Oh, shit it just hit me! Little momma named Tina."

Tone felt his blood pressure rising. *Is this nigga serious?*

"Nigga, do me a favor? Don't ever speak on Tina again like dat. She off limits playboy," Tone said like a savage. Dennis had a smirk on his face. *I knew this nigga was sucka stroking.*

"Yeah aight! I got you, homeboy." Dennis hung up the phone. What was so special about Tina? Dennis couldn't figure it out.

Diary

Tina was excited about having her graduation party in her hood. Everyone pretended to be excited for her, but she heard the rumors over the years.

"She ain't gone be shit."

"She probably gone be like the rest of these hoes with no daddy. Barefoot and pregnant."

The odds were stacked against her, but she was making it out the hood. Keisha and Nikki were so excited for her. They called her several times to make sure she was going to be on time for the party.

"You better be on time, girl!" Keisha said in her parental voice.

"You must be crazy if you think I'm gone be late to my own party. Now, get off my phone so I can get ready!" Tina slammed the phone down.

Tina hopped in the shower and blasted Mary J. Blige through her speakers. Tina jumped out of the shower and slipped on her new dress from C'est La Vie. Tina had bought this pink, hip hugging strapless dress. *Girl, you are so pretty,* she thought as she stared at her figure in the mirror. Her hair had grown so much from wearing braids; the wrap hung below her waist.

"Ok, let's get on our grown woman shit! I'm gone throw on these strappy heels." Tina glanced down at the Donna Karen Shoes.

She rushed out of the house and jumped into her graduation gift. Uncle Joe had gifted her a Chrysler Cherokee.

"I'm that girl now!" Tina shouted as she drove through the hood.

On her way to the party, she stopped to pick up some drinks at Rock's.

"Let's get this party started!

When she stepped inside of Rock's, it was like jaws dropped. Guys were whistling and yelling at her. "Damn, baby girl out cold." She loved the attention, but she was also on a mission. *Now girl don't fuck around and be late.* Tina was rushing; she almost knocked somebody over.

"Shit, I'm sorry!" Tina apologized. She looked up, and the eyes caught her by surprise.

It was Tone. Tina's heart raced like the day she hid from him in that dark alley. She didn't know how to respond or how he would react. It had been months since they had seen each other.

"Bae." Tone felt impulsive, so he grabbed her. He rubbed her hair. *Damn, this girl is so beautiful, man.*

Tina mustered up the strength to utter words. "Hey bae!" She couldn't believe the words she allowed to come out of her mouth.

Hey bae? Seriously, girl did you really just say that."

"Bae, you look so good. Yo pretty ass eyes……Yo hair…….Yo body……Them sexy ass toes." Tone was studying every part of her body.

 It was like they were the only two in the store. Tone leaned in and kissed her softly on the lips.

This nigga got on that damn Versace Blue Jeans cologne. You know that's a bitch weakness.

"Well damn, love birds!" Dennis interrupted.

Where did this nigga come from? Tina thought to herself.

"This my baby, man. I should've married her ass." Tone looked at Dennis.

The word *married* hit Tina hard and that was when she remembered the nigga was already married. She didn't like it, but she couldn't fight the thoughts. *Did he say he wish he married me though? I'm his baby?* His words conflicted Tina. Tone had a tight grip on her too.

Tina realized she needed to go before she missed her own damn graduation party. *Girl, see how this nigga knock you off your square,* Tina replied in her head.

"Bae, it was good to see you, but I have to go though. I'm having my graduation party tonight," Tina said in a soft tone as she peeled back from his embrace.

"Word! Yo shit today, bae? Damn, a nigga really proud of you." Tone was smiling so hard you could see them damn black gums.

"I knew you could do that shit. That's what's up." Tone smiled harder.

"Thank you." Tina blushed. She forgot how much this man could hype her up. He was so proud of her. Tone reached into his pocket and gave her a knot of hundred-dollar bills.

"Grab whatever you want. It's on me, baby." He smiled. Tina smiled from ear to ear.

Tone and Dennis packed her truck with alcohol. They exchanged numbers and agreed to meet after the party. Tina was adamant about him not coming to the party. Secretly, she didn't want anyone to know they were back talking. They kissed again and Tina gawked at him.

"I'm gone hit you after I make this run," he said as he closed her door. Tina raced off to the party.

Now look? We late!

She was so happy to see Tone, but she also felt upset. *Why do I let this man get to me like this?*

When she arrived, everyone bombarded her with questions.

"Girl, where have you been? We bout ready to cut the cake without you?" Freaky Sheila, Uncle Joe's special friend, nagged her.

"I had got caught by a train. Man, it went past then backed up again. I'm sorry ya'll!" Tina said with puppy dog eyes. She had to lie because she needed this to be a secret.

You gone look stupid telling everyone about Tone and he break your heart again. These damn inner thoughts kept taking over. The party was jumping, and she put her energy into the party.

"Dance contest!!" Keisha yelled. Keisha walked over the speaker and cranked up the music. Keisha and Nikki did such a good job with the party. Tina celebrated hard and enjoyed every minute. She was partying so hard that she didn't hear her phone.

When Tina went for another cup of alcohol, she dropped her phone. *Damn, who is this calling me like crazy?* When she called back, she noticed the change in his tone from the store.

"I guess you was all up in some nigga face and couldn't answer," Tone snapped.

"Oh, you trying to get hung up on," Tina snapped back. *You can miss me with the bullshit!*

"My bad, bae. Just trying to see you and shit." Tone checked himself.

Tina said in a tipsy voice, "Fuck it, come scoop me then. She gave him the address and hung up the phone. Tina made plans to sneak out of the party.

***

When Tone pulled up, he could tell she was tipsy. Tina stumbled to the car with her heels in her hand.

Ok new money! I see you.

Immediately, the new car smell engulfed her. Tone was dripping in diamonds.

"Damn, you smell good!" she said as she slid in the car and Tone took off. Tina started climbing over into the driver's seat.

"Bae, what you doin?" Tone asked. Tina started sucking on his ear and rubbing on his face.

"Hey daddy!" she said.

Tone's body felt like it was going into shock. *What is she doing?* Tone was trying to drive but she was acting wild.

Tina pulled her dress down and slipped out her titty. She started flicking her nipples with her tongue. *I want you daddy.* She did some trick and slowly slipped his dick out his shorts. Tina slowly caressed the shaft and circled it with her tongue.

"Ummm," she moaned in ecstasy.

"You wanna wanna go to the room," Tone stuttered. Tone's body wasn't ready for what was happening. *Nigga stop her or we gone cum.* Tone was fighting back the urge to nut.

Tina wouldn't stop sucking until she took every drop down her throat. She slowly came up and sucked on his lips. She was performing like a leading actress in a movie.

"Get in the backseat!" Tone snapped as he grabbed a fist full of hair and ass.

Nigga you gotta make her pay for this or you gone look like a sucka, Tone thought.

He thrusted every inch inside her wet pussy. It felt so good …so moist….so warm. It was like a welcome home party. Tina screamed, "Daddy!" Tone was in heaven, but he couldn't hold back.

"Fuckkkkkkkk!" he yelled. Tone bit her back and cum flowed like a river.

He screamed. "I love you." Tina was drunk, but she heard the words. *What did he just say?*

Tone sat in the backseat in silence.

My, My, My

Ever since that night, Tina was jonesing like Pookie on New Jack City.

Singing………Babyyyyyyyyyy…..My, My, My!!!!!!!!

 Tina was right back at the crack house feening for another hit. She picked up the phone to call Keisha and Nikki to tell them the good news, but they weren't so forgiving.

"Ain't that nigga married?" Keisha snapped.

"Right, he be on some bullshit. He constantly coming in and out your life," Nikki snapped back.

He loves me. They don't know shit about how he makes me feel. "Bye bitches!" Tina slammed the phone down. *I'm not trying to hear that shit today.*

Tina picked the phone back up and dialed Tone's number. It didn't ring long before he picked it up.

"Wassup, ma?" Tone said in a soft voice.

"Hey, bae!" she replied in a sexy tone. They talked for a hot second because he was on the block.

"Let's hook up tonight. Meet me at Ma Dukes crib. We gone do it up, baby!" Tone said.

I do not want this to end. I'm in love with this man. I have to grab something sexy to wear for bae. Maybe he done with wifey. He must be done because he got a lot of free time now. Tina was trying to convince herself.

Tina pushed back her thoughts for the moment and stopped by one of the flyest boutiques on the eastside of Detroit. All the fly girls shopped at Days Boutique. Tina spotted some girls from the hood there soon as she stepped through the door.

"Hey, Tina boo! Congratulations again, girl!" a girl from the hood yelled.

"Thank you, momma." Tina blew fake air kisses. Tina was browsing the store when she found some curvy Parasuco jeans and crop top.

"Yep, these jersey dresses will do too." Tina grabbed a few dresses just in case she needed a backup. When she got to the register, this fine Hershey, dark chocolate nigga walked up to her. She was trying to avoid eye contact.

"You are beautiful!" He had a voice like Barry White.

"Thank you!" Tina said, looking out the corner of her eye.

"You shop here a lot?" the guy asked her as he leaned on the counter.

Ok, what the fuck do you want? She couldn't understand why she hadn't cussed his ass out yet. *My man will kill yo ass if he sees you talking to me.*

"I'm just picking up a few things." Tina tried to brush him off. The stranger was not letting up. "I see you got a lot of bags. I can walk you to your car," he said as he grabbed her bags. *Bitch, what if he trying to steal your shit? What if he a killer.*

For some reason, Tina was thinking logically but acting a fool. It didn't seem like he was going away so she let the stranger walk her to her truck.

"I have my own delivery company. I'm just here making some drop offs. My driver took the day off," he informed her. *Ok working man.*

"Do you think I can call you sometime?" he asked with that smooth voice.

"Maybe! But I don't even know your name though?" Tina replied.

"My name is Vaughn, beautiful. Nice to meet you, Tina," he spoke.

"How you know my name?" She looked in fear.

"Relax! I saw the name on the debit card." He smiled.

"Oh ok!" She lightened up a little. She forgot she was flashing her new Baby Phat Rush card Uncle Joe got her for graduation.

"Hope to see you again." Vaughn smiled as he walked away.

Tina got in the car and watched her "new friend" walk off.

Ok, Vaughn! She smiled to herself.

***

Tina stared at Vaughn's number on the paper.

Vaughn is cute, but we already got a man. Tone would kill me.

Tina heard the phone ringing and started smiling. She spotted Tone's number flashing across the caller id.

"Hey, bae!" She smiled.

"Hey, bae? Where you at?" he asked in a frustrated tone.

Tina hadn't realized she was running late.

"What the fuck you doing?" he yelled into the phone.

"I'm on my way, bae. I'm about………" Tina heard the phone slam. *Did this nigga just hang up in my face?*

Tina knew Tone was pissed, but she was pissed too.

"It ain't my fault you can't be on the damn block. Stupid ASS!" Tina was hot.

He ain't never on some chill shit. Fuck it! It don't hurt to have a conversation.

"Let me call Vaughn fine ass," Tina said as she grabbed the piece of paper with his number on it.

"Hello," Vaughn said in a deep tone.

"Hi, It's Tina," she said bashfully.

"To be honest, I didn't think you were going to call. I'm happy you did though," he replied.

They talked on the phone for hours. Vaughn's conversation was refreshing. He didn't have any kids but most importantly, he didn't have a damn WIFE.

You Will Know

Tina wanted to do things differently, so she didn't allow Vaughn to come over for months. She also had to make sure it wasn't another Red in disguise. The safest way to get to know him was through their phone conversations. When Tina shared with Vaughn that she was starting school at Wayne State in a few weeks, he seemed more excited than her.

"Ok, beautiful, let me at least take you out to celebrate." Vaughn practically begged.

"Hmm, man I don't know." Tina hesitated.

"I tell you what, we can meet in public. We can drive separate cars. I will even let you hold my driver's license," he spoke.

Girl how we gone move on if we never get out? Tina thought to herself.

"Ok, I'm gone tell you now, I do fight," Tina spoke harshly.

"Good thing I'm a lover not a fighter. You in good hands with me," Vaughn said in a serious tone. "Let's do this, beautiful." Vaugh remembered how much Tina enjoyed being a big kid.

"We can go to Michigan Fun Center and drive the go-karts," Vaughn suggested.

Damn, he remembers I like go-karts.

"I'm looking forward to seeing you, Vaughn." Tina hung up the phone and started singing. *Whatta man.. Whatta man,,What a mighty good man.*

A few hours later, Tina made her way to the Michigan Fun Center. She was a little nervous because she was running a few minutes behind, but Vaughn was waiting at the front door. Tina rushed out of her truck.

"Hey, I'm so sorry I'm running late," she said nervously.

"Hey, gorgeous!" Vaughn smiled. "It's all good. I'm just happy to see you."

Tina let out a sigh. "Thank you."

 Vaughn grabbed her hand and walked her into the arcade. She was a little caught off guard that he was such a gentleman.

"You know I'm nice but I'm nice on the court too. Let's get this basketball in first." Tina did a hooping gesture.

"I like you, but I'm not gone take it easy on you because you're pretty." Vaughn did a move like he was Michael Jordan.

"We shall see, buddy!" Tina gave Vaughn a playful push. Hours had passed and they were the last two in the arcade.

"Man, the arcade empty." Tina looked at Vaughn.

"I'm hungry. Let's grab some food." She looked at Vaughn with this innocent look.

"I got you!" He grabbed her hand and led her to his car.

"But I need to see your ID first. I don't even know you like that," she spoke.

"Now you know that's not a problem." Vaughn opened his wallet and passed her his driver's license. *Damn, I wonder who hurt this girl,* he thought.

"Thank you kindly." Tina now felt a sense of comfort getting into his car.

"You good, beautiful?" He noticed Tina was gazing out the window. She was deep in her thoughts.

"I'm sorry, luv! I'm good," Tina replied. *Girl, what the hell you doing? Why you calling this man, luv? You don't even know him like that.*

When they arrived at the restaurant, Tina was awe struck. "Wow, this is a nice place." She smiled at Vaughn.

They were laughing the whole time. Tina couldn't believe how much he was making her smile.

Vaughn paid for the bill and took Tina back to her truck. He gave her the softest hug and forehead kiss.

Not the forehead kiss! We go stupid when a nigga do this.

***

Ever since the day they met, their time together was priceless. They were now going on their one-year anniversary.

This man is everything, she thought as she sat at her desk. The phone rang at her desk.

73

"Hello, This is Miss Jones," Tina said in her corporate voice.

"Hey, baby! Calling to let you know how proud I am of you getting this new job. Did you get your flowers?" Vaughn asked.

Before Tina could reply, a man from FTD Florist walked in with the most beautiful yellow bouquet of flowers.

"Baby, I don't know what to say. I mean thank you," Tina replied with reddened cheeks.

"It's only the beginning. See you later tonight." Vaughn hung up the phone. Tina had to call her cousins at work to let them know.

"Girl, this man. Call Nikki on the three-way," Tina spoke into the phone.

"Girl, hold on…" Keisha clicked over and called Nikki.

"What he do now, girl?" Nikki asked. They were cracking up on the phone. Tina almost forgot she was at work.

"I bet you glad you left Tone alone, huh?" Nikki asked.

"I'm sorry girl, bad connection." Tina started imitating static.

"Say what now? Tone who? Tone what?" Tina played clueless. Tina hadn't spoken to Tone in almost a year now. She didn't even have the desire to call him. It felt so weird to be in this space. *It is what it is,* she thought.

"Let me get back to work before I get fired like Craig on Friday." The girls laughed.

"Bye ya'll!" Tina said. Tina hung up the phone and went back to work. She felt so good inside. She was at work imitating SWV. *You're always on my mind....thinking bout ya... thinking bout ya.*

***

Tina grabbed Vaughn's arm as they walked through the park. "Baby, I think it's time you meet my Uncle Joe. Especially, if we plan on moving in together. I have to get his approval first." Tina gave him a serious look.

"You already know I've been waiting to meet him. I told you that before. I been waiting on you this whole time." Vaughn returned the look.

"I know...I know, baby. I had to make sure it was real first. Now, I feel like it is," Tina replied. Tina pulled out her cellphone and gave Uncle Joe a quick call.

"Hey Unk! Now, you know it's before seven. I don't have a lot of minutes, but I wanted to tell you something real quick. I want you to meet Vaughn," Tina said nervously.

"Alright, baby girl. Bring the boy by this weekend. Unk got to go now. I only got sixty minutes left on this damn phone card," Uncle Joe said. *Why is this man still using a damn prepaid cellphone?*

"Alright Unk, love you." Tina rushed off the phone.

Tina turned to Vaughn. "Alright, we can go by his house on Saturday."

Vaughn kissed her forehead. "Cool, baby."

Vaughn grabbed her hand and led her to the car. Tina felt ready but a part of her still questioned if Vaughn really loved her. *Is this man too good to be true?*

***

"I can smell the ribs from outside," Tina said as she stood in front of the house.

"Uncle be throwing down like that?" Vaughn asked as he inhaled the smell of Open Pit BBQ.

"Oh, you gone be hooked," Tina replied as she walked toward the backyard. Tina ran over to Uncle Joe and hugged him.

"Uncle, meet my boyfriend, Vaughn." She blushed. "Vaughn this my Uncle Joe."

"Pleasure to meet you, sir." Vaughn extended his arm for a handshake. Joe gave Tina a look that said he was impressed.

"Come have a seat, young man. Get comfortable." Uncle Joe ushered Vaughn to the lawn chair.

Uncle Joe walked over to the grill so he could turn his ribs over. "You not like them other knuckleheads she use to date. I wouldn't even say date, I guess messing wit."

"Ok Uncle, please don't embarrass me," she said, walking over to grab her a hot dog. "Oh, you burnt them just how I like'em." They ate some BBQ and played spades.

Vaughn and Uncle Joe both had a love of cars. They seemed to bond as they exchanged stories about their favorite old school cars.

Oh, he really feeling him, Tina thought as she watched Uncle Joe offer Vaughn some of his favorite cognac.

"Baby girl, let me holla at you for a second." Uncle Joe pointed toward the house. Uncle Joe sat on the couch lined in plastic.

"Vaughn seems like a good wholesome young man. If anything happens to me, I need someone I can trust to watch after you." Uncle Joe's voice started to crackle.

"What you mean, Unk?" Tina asked.

"I don't want to spoil the mood, but I got that damn cancer. They said I got pancreatic cancer or whatever you call it." Tears formed in Uncle Joe's eyes.

Wait, what does this mean? Are you leaving me? Tina's thoughts flashed to all the times she didn't have anyone, and Uncle Joe was there. He was the one that rescued her from Nasty Nancy's house. It was him that was at her graduation. He was her family.

Who will care for me now? Tina sat, sulking in silence.

Emotional

Tina was slumped over in Vaughn's lap and cried until she couldn't breathe. Uncle Joe's health was rapidly declining.

"This shit is so fucked up, man." Tina tried to speak in between sobbing. "I can't believe he been going through chemo for six months man."

"The one person that stepped up in my life Why him, God?" Tina wiped the snot from her nose.

"I know, baby." Vaughn kissed her forehead.

"God don't make mistakes though," Vaughn said with conviction.

"Oh really? What about when he allowed me to be molested? Cussed out? Lied on?" Tina sadness was turning into anger.

"Baby, I'm not saying none of that was right. I just need you to trust him or trust me at least." Vaughn grabbed her hand and started to pray. *Now what is that gone do? Vaughn, I NEED YOU TO MAN UP RIGHT NOW!*

"Do you hear me? Are you even listening?" Tina yelled. "I hate when you be nonchalant like my feelings don't matter. I'm out!" Tina stood up to walk toward the door.

Vaughn ran toward her and grabbed her waist. "I got you baby. You safe with me. I keep telling you that. You got to learn to trust someone and let me love you." He hugged her tighter.

"I just been through so much shit. Vaughn, I'm scared," Tina confessed through tears.

***

Tina, Keisha, and Nikki altered shifts with Uncle Joe. Tina was trying to stay sane as she maneuvered through her new reality. *Why can't I just have a cool life with no bullshit?* Tina thought as she waited for Keisha to take her shift.

"Baby girl, how did you afford to pay for an in-home nurse," Uncle Joe said in a whisper.

"Uncle, I didn't pay for a nurse. It must've been yo kids or one of them little freaks from your past." Tina tried to make him laugh or better yet herself. Tina jumped when she heard the screen door open.

"Hey ya'll!" Keisha said with a concerned look.

"Cousin, can I talk to you outside?" Keisha looked at Tina.

"Yeah, we can go talk in my car." Tina walked toward the door. "Ok, what's up?"

"Girl, I got some bad news," Keisha said.

"Can't be worse than this shit." Tina sighed.

"Tone's momma got murdered." Keisha started to ramble.

79

"Wait….Wait…Wait! You said what?" Tina was not comprehending what she was being told.

"Yes girl, she got murdered." Keisha sniffled. "Dennis called me and told me." *Tone would die for that lady, man. This is fucked up. But what the fuck that got to do with me?*

"I gotta go." Tina leaned over and hugged Keisha. "I love you, cuz."

"Look, I know ya'll ain't talked in a minute, but Dennis said Tone want to see you. He heard about my dad too and he wanted to talk."

"Look, I gotta go home." Tina rushed off. Tina drove home in a daze. The Alpine Stereo blasted Xscape. *As I stand here contemplating on the right thing to decide…………..Who Can I run to? Who can I run to… to fill this empty space?*

***

Tina mentioned to Vaughn what Keisha told her earlier. In Vaughn's eyes, it was him who helped her to recover from Tone. He hated to hear about somebody getting murdered, but he didn't understand why Tina cared.

Fuck that nigga! Vaughn thought.

"I haven't called Keisha since I left," Tina said. "Do you mind if I have some privacy?"

"Not at all, baby. I'm gone drive to the city and grab you some Robert's." Vaughn flashed her a smile.

"Baby, you already know that's my favorite. Thank you." Tina stood up and kissed Vaughn on the cheek. "You make me smile."

"That's all I wanna do, baby." Vaughn stood up to grab his keys. Tina waited until she heard Vaughn pull out of the driveway before she called Keisha.

"Hey, girl!" Keisha started spilling all the details of what happened.

"Girl, how could his daddy do that to her."

"Cousin, you have to call Tone. You know he probably messed up after this," Keisha urged.

"You know I'm with Vaughn. Girl, I can't do that. I don't even know how to approach Tone about this. I haven't talked to him in so long." Tina was battling so many emotions.

She secretly felt bad for Tone. His momma was the one person he really loved. *I know how it feels to not have a momma.*

"Give me some time to think about it," Tina said before she hung up the phone.

Killing Me Softly

Alright girl, I'm gone take one for the team, Keisha thought as she stood in front of the funeral home. "I got my own shit with my daddy. I'm gone be in and out." Keisha gave herself a pep talk before walking in. Keisha spotted Tone and Dennis near the casket.

Damn man! Her hands started sweating. Dennis walked over to Keisha first.

"What's up, girl?" Dennis kissed her cheek. "You look good, girl."

"Boy, you better stop. This ain't the time nor the place for us to go back and forth. I gave my cousin the message like you asked me to," Keisha replied.

Tone spotted Keisha then looked around. Keisha knew he was looking for Tina, but she came solo to pay her respects.

"I'm sorry, man," Keisha said with tears in her eyes.

Tone gave Keisha the biggest hug. She could tell he was trying to hold back the tears. They kicked it for a minute before Keisha broke the ice. She already knew what was up.

"Tina, wanted me to tell you she sends her condolences." Keisha looked at him.

"Where my girl at, man? I need her, man," Tone said with the most sincerity he'd ever had in his life. "Take my number man and tell her to call me."

Keisha knew she was gone have to grant this man his wishes. Shit, the man just lost his momma.

***

Tina looked at Tone's number for hours. Keisha had given her the message. Tina was mad about everything that happened in the past but hell she was in a relationship now. *Why shit always have to be so complicated?* Tina battled with whether she should attend the funeral tomorrow, call, or just send him a silent prayer.

This shit is bothering me. I can't even sleep. Is he okay? I can't believe he said he need me. But where were you when I needed you, Tone?

"Let's just send our condolences," Tina said out loud and called the number.

Damn, do I leave a message or just hang up? If he answers, what am I gonna say?

"Fuck it!" Tina yelled. She decided to leave a voicemail. "Hey, bae, it's me. I'm so sorry to hear about momma. Call me if you need anything," Tina said softly. *Hey, bae? Girl what the fuck was that about?* Tina went to bed, but she understood what she had to do. *I gotta do, what I gotta do. Tone is my first love. I do owe him that much.*

After a restless night, Tina decided to pay her respects. *If I go early, nobody will see me. Maybe I can just sign the guest book, so he knows I at least came by,* she thought.

"I'm not trying to run into his damn wife either. I would hate for it to be two funerals if she came at me crazy." Tina huffed.

***

When Tina got to the funeral home, the air felt crisp. It was eerily cold. Tina wore a knee-length, black sweater dress with black patent leather pumps. Her hair was tucked nicely in her signature sleek bun sun kissed with some honey blonde highlights.

"Alright girl, you got this. Just breathe!" She gave herself a pep talk.

When she walked in, she immediately spotted Dennis. *Fuck man! I hope Tone is not here yet.* Dennis walked over to her and gave her a hug.

"You look good, girl. Glad you came to pay yo respects. Tone would be happy to see you," Dennis said.

"Oh! I'm not staying, and you know why. But I couldn't not come and say my goodbyes," Tina said as she tried to move past Dennis. Tina made her way inside to view the body. Her heart became heavier as she looked down at his mom. *How will he live without her?*

Tina rushed out before the family was scheduled to walk in.

***

Tone was sitting in his garage when he hit the blunt. He needed Mary Jane to take the pain away. It was late and WJLB was playing the slow jams on the radio.

I'm never keeping secrets and I'm never telling lies..

"What the fuck was this nigga Babyface talkin' about?" Tone laughed. *I wonder if that shit really worked for you nigga.*

Tone was still listening to Babyface crying about never telling secrets when he picked up his cellphone. He had about thirty messages. "I guess I might as well listen to these muthafuckas." He sighed.

Most of them were people calling to express their condolences. He went through the messages quickly until he heard a familiar voice. "Hey, bae!" Tina's voice spoke softly through the phone. Her voice was like an angel. His heart started beating and that warm feeling came back. That feeling he had when he met her on the block way back when.

"Fuck it! Let me call her." Tone pressed 1 to dial the caller back.

Ring...Ring...Ring...

***

Tina quickly picked up the phone. *Who the hell calling this late? Did something happen to Uncle Joe?*

"Hey, bae!" It was the voice she fell in love with years ago. The man that she gave her heart to. *Is it really him, Lord?* Tina's heart pulsated.

Vaughn was in a deep sleep, and she couldn't let either of these niggas know about one another.

"Hey, hold on one second," she whispered. Tina slipped out the bed and went to the garage. She sat in her car and turned on WJLB. *Oh! They playing the jams.* Tina smiled.

"Hey, bae? How have you been?" Tina asked.

Tone couldn't lie.

"Bae, I'm fucked up! I need to see you. My girl gone, man," Tone said in a cracked voice.

Is he crying? Tina couldn't wrap her mind around this moment. *He sounds so hurt man,* she thought to herself.

"Bae, I fucked up. I hurt you and I wasn't a man about my shit. I got another kid. I never told you when I got married. I was acting like a little ass boy. After losing moms, I realize you the only love I got left." Tone was finally honest. *I guess this nigga, Babyface was right. I ain't never keeping secrets or never telling lies.* He took a swig of Hennessy. *Let's see how this shit works out for us playboy.*

Tina listened as Tone poured out his heart. It was like the apology she had waited years to receive.

Tina kept thinking about the conversation she had with Tone. She told him that she would meet up with him soon. *Maybe this is closure. Maybe it's just a meeting between two friends. Yep, he is just a friend that needs me. I don't know what the fuck I'm doing but I'm going,* Tina thought.

"Hey, beautiful!" Vaughn kissed Tina's forehead. He came into the kitchen and interrupted her thoughts.

"I'm going to hang out. Here goes some money to grab you something to eat or we can meet up later if you want," Vaughn said.

"It's cool, luv. I'm gone meet up with Keisha." Tina hated lying but the shit was necessary right now. She had to get to Tone.

Tina waited until he left then peered through the blinds until she saw Vaughn's car pull out of the garage. *Let me put some music on,* she thought.

"You betta sang Johnny!" Tina was dancing to New Edition in her closet while looking for a cute, knitted dress. "Oh, this would be super cute and comfortable. I can wear my thigh boots too." Tina smiled. Tina grabbed her cellphone to call Tone.

"Hey, I should be there in about an hour," she said in a firm voice.

"Baby, I'm waiting on you whenever you get here," Tone spoke softly into the phone.

Who in the fuck is this? He talking real soft and shit. His patience is always short and now he waiting on me. "Alright, bae! See you soon." Tina felt weird. *How is this shit about to turn out?*

***

When she pulled up on the block, she saw a crowd of niggas. "Fuck, I don't want anybody to see me. Shit!!! I can't back out now though!" she screamed. *I can't believe these niggas still hanging out on the block.*

Tina got out of the car smelling like Pear Glace from Victoria Secret. Her hair was flowing like she was a girl in a rap video. She put a little switch in her hips as she walked up the driveway.

"DAMN!" She heard one of the niggas yell out.

Tone came from around the house. He gave them that familiar deadly look. *Yeah, that nigga still don't play about me.*

Tone grabbed Tina tightly around the waist and led her down into the basement of his momma's house.

Bitch, I thought we was coming over as a friend for support. Huh hoe?

Tina collapsed into his arms. It felt like their souls needed one another. They just held each other.

"Luv you, bae!" Tone kissed her on the forehead.

"I love you too." Tina let the words slip from her mouth.

They spent the next two hours talking and holding hands. Tina felt like she was in high school again when he looked at her. She loved Vaughn but the feeling Tone gave her was different.

The next few days were rough. Tina was feeling uneasy after seeing Tone. Tone would call her every day and check on her. He would tell her he loved her before they hung up the phone. She always rushed him off before replying. *I wonder if he really changed this time.*

Tina didn't want a repeat of the past. She had created this new life with Vaughn. Vaughn was her safety. He wasn't a liar or a cheater. Tina still entertained both lives by switching from the block to Vaughn. Tone was turning into the man she always wanted. *Bae is a gangster and a gentleman.*

Vaughn threw her for a loop one Sunday night. She was on her way to the block when he started calling her back-to-back. "My Man" kept flashing across her phone.

"Damn, I gotta answer. He gone think something wrong if I don't." Tina mustered up the courage to answer.

"Hey baby, where you at?" Vaughn quizzed.

"Umm..I just had to go grab some food for Uncle Joe," she lied.

"I got a surprise for you. Can you be back around eight?" Vaughn asked.

"Of course, baby. Anything for you," Tina said in a sexy voice.

"I can't wait to see you." Vaughn blushed. Today was one of those days where she had a heavy heart from lying. *Is it really worth it?*

Bonus Track-Heavy Heart

Tina was on her way to the block when Tony! Toni! Tone! came on the radio. *We don't need nobody else…just me and you…Just the two!*

"Damn, this my shit!" Tina started singing. The song made her think about all the moments between her and Tone. The day she met him at Rock's and fell for him. He was the one that took her virginity. Yet, he was the one that broke her heart by marrying someone else. But when she was around him, she couldn't shake the butterflies in her stomach. No matter who she dated, she thought about Tone. Well, that was until Vaughn came into her life. *God, what do you really want me to do? Who do you want me to be with?* Tina questioned.

Tony! Toni! Tone! was still blasting when she pulled up on the block. She spotted Tone's Cadillac and pulled up behind him. As soon as she stepped out of the car, she felt his eyes all over her.

"Bae, you so pretty!" Tone said. "You my dream girl." He couldn't stop staring at her. Tina felt like he was looking into her soul or something. Tone leaned in and kissed her on the forehead.

"You want something to drank from the sto?" he asked.

"Yeah, you know I want a lil nip nip." She laughed. *Maybe some wine will help me take the edge off.* Tone reached down and grabbed his cd case. He browsed through the catalog until he found the P.M. Dawn CD.

Is it my turn to wish you were lying here? I tend to dream you when I'm not sleeping. The cd started skipping........*If I have to sacrrrrrrifice.*

"Damn!" Tone said. A hurling scream muffled the music.

POP…POP…POPPPP…

Bullets riddled the car like fireworks. The bullets sent fiery lava into Tina's chest. She felt her chest cave in as she slumped over into Tone's lap. Her body felt like she was on fire.

She was hit! She struggled to lift her body up as she looked into Tone's eyes.

Tone was hit! He was struggling to speak. *"Luuuuv you, ma!"*

"Bae, I…………" All she heard were her thoughts. *What about Vaughn? What about me……me?*

Tina struggled to talk when everything faded to black.

**Radio Plays* Is there anything that I would not do? Cause I'd die without you. I'd die without you.*

***

Vaughn called and called. *Man, something ain't right.* Vaughn was going to propose to her tonight. It was time he made it official. Vaughn thought it was Tina calling back, but it was Keisha.

"I just got a call from the hospital. Daddy not gone make it much longer," Keisha cried.

"Tina told me she was taking him some food. What you mean?" Vaughn said nervously.

Keisha turned around and saw the headlines on the news.

News Reporter: **Drive-by shooting takes place on the Eastside of Detroit. One person was fatally shot. We have one fatality.**

Keisha's heart dropped when she saw Tone's Cadillac.

Black Hearts

HisStory

Coming Soon